The Wonderful World of Disney

WALT DISNEY

SLEEPING BEAUTY

Twin Books

DERRYDALE BOOKS
New York

In a kingdom long ago, the Queen gave birth to a baby girl. Since the Queen and King Stefan had waited many years for a child, they were very happy indeed. They ordered an enormous feast, and invited everyone to come celebrate. The neighboring King Hubert attended with his young son, Prince Phillip, who would someday marry the little princess and unite their kingdoms. Three good fairies, Flora, Fauna, and Merryweather, came to the party to present gifts to the baby, Princess Aurora.

Flora granted the baby the gift of beauty, and Fauna had just given her the gift of song, when suddenly there was a terrifying flash of lightning.

The wicked fairy, Maleficent, appeared.
"Why was I not invited to this party?" she
demanded angrily. She glared at the King
and Queen. "Well, I have a special gift
for your daughter."

Maleficent pointed to the baby. "Before your sixteenth birthday, little princess, you will prick your finger on the spindle of a spinning wheel, and you will die!" Then the evil fairy vanished as quickly as she had come.

Merryweather stepped forward. "I
cannot undo the evil spell, but I can
soften it," she said. "The princess will not
die, but will fall into a deep sleep, from
which only True Love's Kiss can awaken
her." Then the three fairies offered to
disguise themselves as peasants and take
the princess into the forest to grow up in
secret.

Sadly, the King and Queen agreed to
the fairies' plan. Although they loved
their little princess dearly, they knew that
with the fairies she would be safe from
Maleficent. The King and Queen watched
from the castle window as the fairies
disappeared into the forest with their baby.

After a long journey, the group arrived at an abandoned cottage.

"This is hardly a place for a princess!" exclaimed Merryweather.

"Sh-h-h!" scolded Flora. "We must never say the word 'princess' again. We are simple peasants, and she is our niece!"

The women named the baby Briar Rose, and gave her all the love and care of real parents. As the years passed, Briar Rose grew into a beautiful young girl. Soon she would be sixteen.

The fairies wanted to prepare a
birthday surprise for Briar Rose, so they
sent her out to pick wild berries. The
princess wandered through the forest,
singing to her animal friends.

A young horseman passed by and heard the sound of her singing. "Who could that be singing so sweetly?" he wondered. "I must find her." He turned his horse and started through the forest, but as they jumped over a log, the young man was brushed off his mount by an overhanging branch.

He landed in a pond, where he stared at his horse in dismay. "No carrots for you tonight," he said jokingly, scrambling out of the water. Then he took off his boots, and hung his cape and hat on a branch to dry.

Meanwhile, Briar Rose spoke wistfully to her animal friends. "My aunts say never to speak to a stranger," she sighed. "But I've disobeyed them. I have spoken to a tall, handsome man—in my dreams."

While Briar Rose sang a song about the love of her dreams, the animals found the clothes the young man had left to dry. They dressed up to surprise Briar Rose.

"Ah, my Prince!" exclaimed Briar Rose as she embraced the owl in the cape. The bunnies hopped about in the boots, and the squirrel held up the hat, as they danced to the beautiful song Briar Rose sang.

Suddenly, a man's voice joined in the
song, and Briar Rose felt her hands
grasped gently. "Don't worry," he said.
"We've already met. I'm the one of your
dreams."

Briar Rose and the man danced, but soon she had to leave. As she ran off she called to the young man to meet her that night at the cottage in the glen.

Back at the cottage, Fauna had been trying to bake her first cake. She had never made a cake without magic.

16

Fauna tried to follow the recipe, but before long she'd made a huge mess. "This doesn't seem to be coming out quite right," she thought.

Then she arranged the cake in layers, but it flopped to one side. When she tried to prop it up, the icing and candles slid down the stick. "Perhaps I should've baked that part, too," she mused.

Flora had been trying to sew Briar Rose a ballgown, but she had been unsuccessful, as well. Suddenly, Merryweather exclaimed, "Briar Rose will be returning soon and we'll never get this right by then. Let's use our magic just this once."

She fetched their magic wands and in a jiffy the house was cleaned, a beautiful ballgown was created and a perfect cake was baked and decorated. It was not a moment too soon.

"Surprise!" shouted the aunts as Briar Rose came in. She was surprised and delighted. "What a wonderful day!" she exclaimed. "First I met my True Love, and now this!"

The aunts were alarmed. When Briar Rose told them of the man in the forest, they explained to her that she was a princess, and that that very day she would be returning to the castle where she'd been born, to marry Prince Phillip.

"You must never see that man again," Flora said.

Briar Rose cried bitterly, for in her heart she loved the man of her dreams whom she'd met in the forest. Sadly, she put on her cape and left the cottage with the fairies to make the long trip home. The four walked in silence, the fairies thinking of what joy Briar Rose had given them and how they would miss her, Briar Rose thinking of her dear aunts and of the man she loved.

Meanwhile, the man in the forest had dashed homeward. "Father!" he cried, as he dismounted and rushed to King Hubert, for he was the King's son, Prince Phillip.

"You must get ready at once," said the King, "for you will meet your bride, Princess Aurora today!"

"Oh, no!" replied the prince. "I'm going to marry a peasant girl I met in the forest. She's wonderful!"

"A peasant?" gasped the King. "I forbid it! Go get ready to meet your bride."

But Phillip sprang onto his horse and galloped away, shouting over his shoulder, "I'm going to meet my bride now, Father, at the cottage in the glen!"

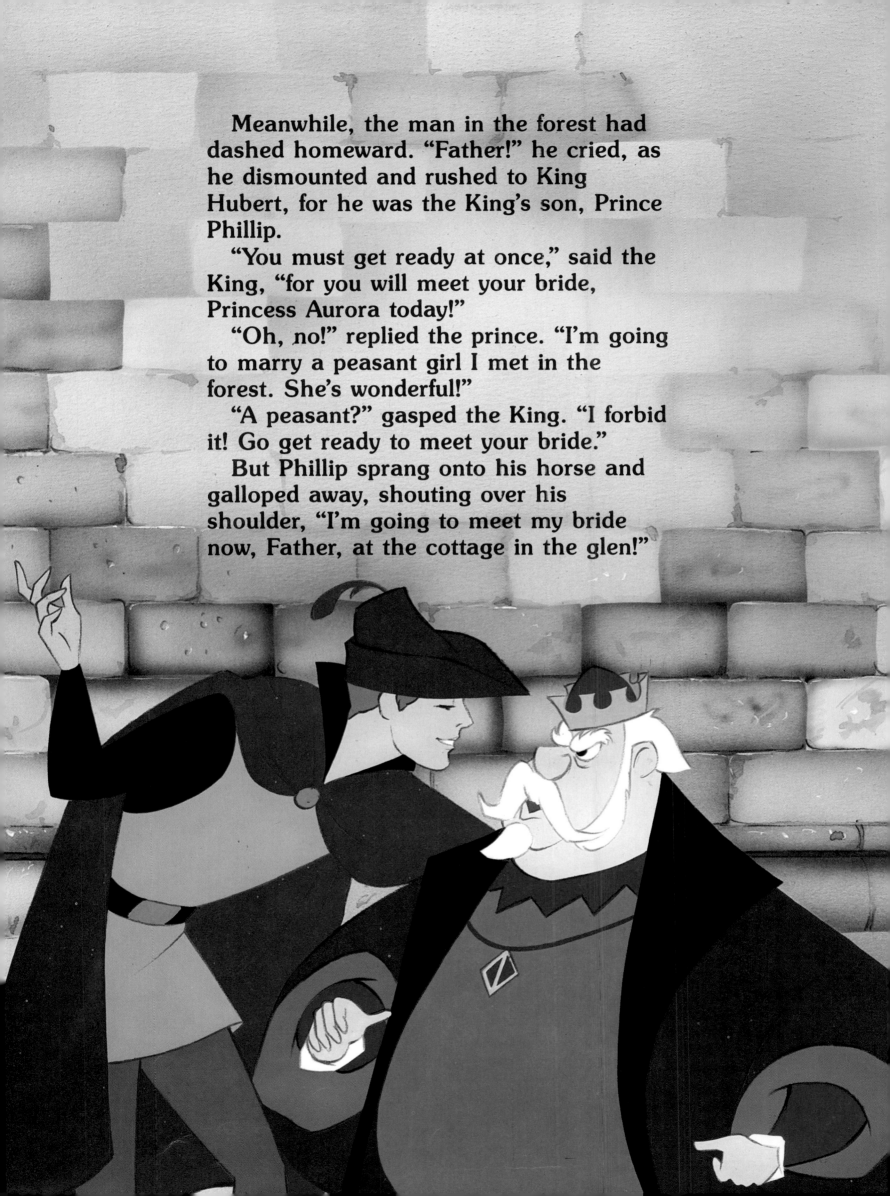

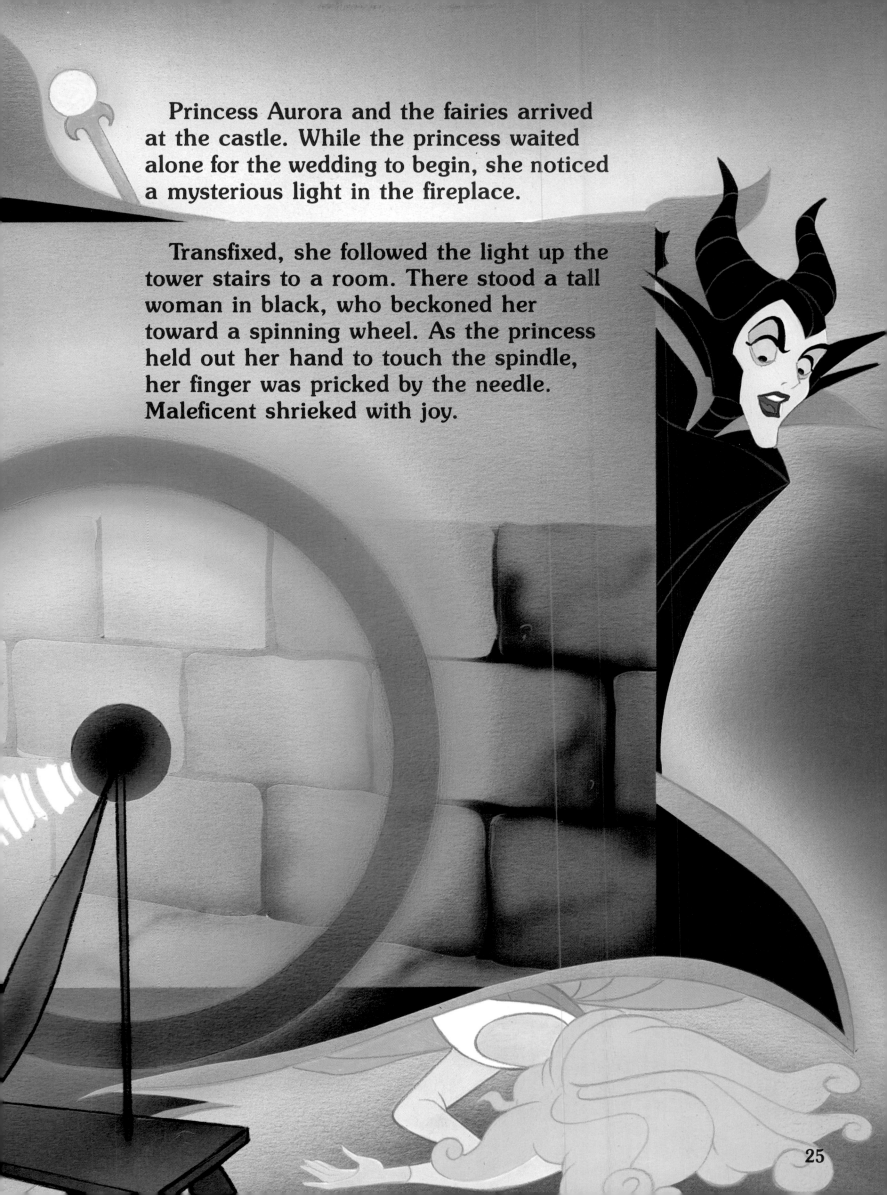

Princess Aurora and the fairies arrived at the castle. While the princess waited alone for the wedding to begin, she noticed a mysterious light in the fireplace.

Transfixed, she followed the light up the tower stairs to a room. There stood a tall woman in black, who beckoned her toward a spinning wheel. As the princess held out her hand to touch the spindle, her finger was pricked by the needle. Maleficent shrieked with joy.

The fairies were horrified when they discovered the fallen princess. Gently, they placed her on a bed.

"What shall we do now?" asked Merryweather. The fairies decided to put everyone in the castle to sleep until the princess' true love could be found.

Just as King Hubert dozed off, Flora heard him tell the sleeping King Stefan that Prince Phillip had gone to meet his bride, a peasant, in the forest.

"A peasant!" cried Flora, realizing at once that the man of the princess' dreams must have been Prince Phillip. The fairies flew in great haste toward the cottage.

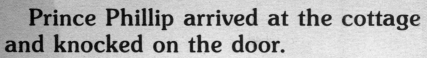

Prince Phillip arrived at the cottage and knocked on the door.

"Come in," replied a sly voice. As he entered the cottage he was attacked by Maleficent's guards, who bound him up with heavy rope.

Maleficent brought the prince to the dungeon of her dark and evil castle.

"I may release you in a hundred years," she said, laughing. "Then we will see how true your love is."

29

As Maleficent spoke she showed the prince a vision
of the fallen princess in her crystal ball, and he realized the girl
in the forest had been none other than Princess Aurora.
    Meanwhile, the fairies had found his hat in the cottage, and
had flown to Maleficent's castle.

When Maleficent left, they appeared to the prince. They explained who they were and freed him from his chains.

"You must go to Aurora at once," instructed Flora. "Only True Love's Kiss can awaken her."

"Here, take this Shield of Virtue," said Flora, waving her wand. A brilliant shield appeared in the prince's hand. "And take this Sword of Truth!" she commanded, as a sword flew into his other hand.

Maleficent's pet raven had discovered the prince escaping. "Caw! Caw!" warned the bird, alerting the guards. Dozens of evil creatures rushed after him, brandishing their weapons. Prince Phillip fought with all his might. His shield and sword were magical, indeed, as his enemies were felled left and right.

He sprang onto his waiting horse and galloped through the gates. Maleficent had heard the commotion, and when she came to her tower and saw the prince fleeing, her heart filled with rage. "I shall not be thwarted!" she screamed, sending a shower of boulders at the prince. His Shield of Virtue deflected the boulders like pebbles as his horse galloped on.

Then Maleficent gathered her evil
powers and cast another spell. A maze of
brambles and thorns a mile thick grew
up around King Stefan's castle. In a
hundred years no man could have made
his way through them. But the prince,
brandishing his Sword of Truth, hacked
them down as he advanced, and before
long the castle lay clear.

Suddenly, Maleficent herself stood in his path, and with a flash of lightning she changed into a monstrous black dragon. "No mere mortal can defeat the power of evil," she hissed. The dragon came forward.

The prince swung his sword and held up his shield, backing away as the dragon advanced. Phillip was no bigger than one of the dragon's horrible claws.

The dragon let out a blazing roar of fire.

The fire deflected off Phillip's shield and hit the brambles, which burst into flames. Phillip swung his sword at the dragon's face, but he couldn't get close enough to strike it.

39

Roaring and snarling, the dragon pushed Phillip back until he stood on the edge of a cliff. The creature's yellow eyes gleamed wickedly as it prepared for the kill.

The dragon reared back to take a mighty breath. Prince Phillip's Sword of Truth sang through the air, and found its mark in the dragon's heart. With a deafening shriek of agony the dragon fell forward, tumbling over the cliff to its death.

The prince hurried to the castle, where he passed the slumbering wedding guests and ascended the stairs. As he entered the tower room where Princess Aurora lay in a death-like sleep, he gasped at her beauty. "It is indeed the woman I love," he whispered. He crossed the floor and gazed at her face.

The prince kissed Aurora tenderly, and the spell was broken.

"It's you!" she cried with joy. The prince and princess, destined for marriage since her birth, gazed at one another in silence. Then the prince explained to her about Maleficent's spell, and what had happened.

Princess Aurora watched the man of her dreams as he spoke. "You are Prince Phillip," she said, smiling. "And you are my bride," he answered.

Meanwhile, the fairies busied themselves awakening everyone. King Hubert and King Stefan awoke with a start. "Dear me," mumbled King Stefan. "The wedding preparations must have tired us. But now we are ready. Let the wedding begin."

King Hubert was about to explain that Prince Phillip refused to marry Aurora, when the couple entered the chamber.

As the prince and princess approached their parents, the crowd watched silently, marveling at Aurora's beauty. The princess curtsied gracefully and the prince bowed.

Then Princess Aurora
looked at her mother for
the first time, and rushed
into her arms.

"You are lovely, my child!"
cried the Queen, hugging
her daughter tightly.

"May we never part
again!" said Aurora.

The two kings smiled at each other, happy that their
kingdoms would be united at last through the marriage of their
children. Then the music began, and Princess Aurora and
Prince Phillip danced together. Hovering on the balcony, the
good fairies Merryweather, Flora and Fauna watched them.
They knew that the prince and princess would have many children,
rule over their kingdom wisely, and live happily ever after.

This 1988 edition published by Derrydale Books,
distributed by Crown Publishers, Inc.,
225 Park Avenue South
New York, New York 10003

Directed by HELENA Productions Ltd.
Image adaptation by Van Gool-Lefevre-Loiseaux

Produced by Twin Books
15 Sherwood Place
Greenwich, CT 06830

Printed and bound in Hong Kong

ISBN 0-517-67009-7

h g f e d c b a

The Wonderful World of Disney